About Alex Gutteridge

I am a Woollyback, which means I was born and brought up in Leicestershire. I still live there with my husband, three children, two cats, one hamster and too many fish to count. I love autumn, skipping and fresh raspberries, and I hate feeling cold, anything to do with maths and spiders.

Witch Wendy flew into my mind one murky November afternoon while sitting in some roadworks on the way to pick up my daughter. The cones were all covered in mud and I thought they looked like witches' hats.

Also by Alex Gutteridge

Pirate Polly Rules the Waves

Look out for

Princess Posy, Knight in Training

Witch * Wendy

Works Her Magic

Alex Gutteridge

Illustrated by Annabel Hudson

MACMILLAN CHILDREN'S BOOKS

Witch Wendy Cats and Hats, *Witch Wendy Broom Broom!* and *Witch Wendy Cat Tricks*
first published as separate titles by Macmillan Children's Books

This omnibus edition published 2004 by Macmillan Children's Books
a division of Macmillan Publishers Limited
20 New Wharf Road, London N1 9RR
Basingstoke and Oxford
www.panmacmillan.com

Associated companies throughout the world

ISBN 0 330 43404 7

A CIP catalogue record for this book is available from
the British Library.

Typeset by Macmillan Publishers Limited
Printed and bound in Great Britain by Mackays of Chatham plc, Kent

Contents

Cats
and
Hats

For Christopher, Nicholas and Emily

Chapter One

Witch Wendy was fed up. It had rained and rained for nights and nights. Everything was covered in mud: her cat Snowflake, her cloak and her hat.

She looked in the mirror. The hat was dirty. It was crumpled and it didn't stand up straight like a witch's hat should.

The point flopped down in front of her
eyes. Even when she wore her special
flying glasses, she couldn't see properly.
This made riding the broomstick a
big problem.

x

4

Last month Wendy had crashed into a tree; last week she had landed in a pond; and last night she had careered into all the other witches and caused a horrible pile-up. They were very cross with her, but there was nothing new about that.

"Somehow," Wendy said to Snowflake, "I need to get a new hat. Perhaps I'll try the hat spell again."

"PLEASE NO!" Snowflake miaowed loudly. "No more horrible hat tricks!" He checked his watch. "If we don't hurry we'll be late for the picnic in the park and Witch Rosemary

will turn us both into frogs again."

Wendy opened the front door. The broomstick was parked outside. Snowflake fixed the picnic basket in the middle and he jumped on the back. The rain had stopped but the sky was very black and there was no hint of the moon.

"You're a clever cat, Snowflake," said Wendy, "and you can see better in the dark than I can. You drive the broomstick tonight."

"I'll have to sit at the front then," said Snowflake.

"Oh no," Wendy said. "You can't do that. It's against the Flyway Code.

Cats must always perch at the back. We'll fly the broomstick backwards!"

"Are cats allowed to fly broomsticks?" asked Snowflake.

"Well, no," grinned Wendy. "It'll be our secret."

"Don't you think Witch Rosemary will smell a bat if we don't crash as usual?" muttered Snowflake.

But Wendy wasn't listening. She was trying very hard to get the Friday night flying spell right first time.

"Broomstick, Broomstick, let's be quick,
we're off to the park for a witches' picnic.
Backwards, backwards, off we go,
come on broomstick,
don't be slow!"

Snowflake strapped on his crash helmet and tightened up his seat belt.

Wendy fixed on her flying glasses and
waved her wand.

"Here we go again," Snowflake murmured as the broomstick zoomed down the garden path towards take-off.

Chapter Two

"YES!" squealed Wendy, bouncing up and down. "We did it first time."

"Will you please sit still," growled Snowflake. "You'll break the broomstick."

"Sorry," said Wendy, "I'll try to be good."

So the witch faced forwards, the broomstick flew backwards and Snow-flake began to enjoy himself. Once or twice he peeped behind him to check Wendy was behaving.

Soon they heard sneaky laughter and rude noises in the distance.

"Watch out! Here comes Witch Wendy and her horrible hat," a voice cackled through the clouds.

"Here comes Witch Rosemary and her horrible cat," muttered Snowflake.

Witch Rosemary glided into view, her hat as tall and straight as a church spire.

"Not found the right hat spell yet, I see?" smirked Rosemary.

"I've nearly got it," lied Wendy, lifting her hat up so she could see the other witches.

"She's talking through her hat!" Witch Harriet jeered. "She shouldn't be allowed out dressed like that."

"Are you sure you can see properly?" asked Witch Primrose.

"Of course I can," said Wendy. "I'm wearing my flying glasses."

"Hmm," Witch Rosemary murmured. "I suppose you can come with us to the park, but BE CAREFUL."

"It's my turn first on the swings this week," Wendy shouted after them as Rosemary, Primrose and Harriet raced away at top speed. "Let's go faster, Snowflake. We'll soon catch them."

"But there are witches all over the place," said Snowflake as lots of shadowy figures filled the sky. "If we go any faster we'll crash."

Wendy wasn't listening.

"Broomstick, broomstick, make it

snappy, if you want this witch to be happy," she chanted.

The broomstick picked up speed and Snowflake put his paws over his eyes.

"Oh, my fearful fur," Snowflake moaned.

"Trust me," said Wendy. "I know what I'm doing."

"I've heard that before," Snowflake groaned.

"I know a short cut to the park," squealed Wendy. "We'll get there before them. Turn left, Snowflake."

Snowflake peeped through one paw.

"I don't think that's a good idea," he shouted.

"Snowflake, who's in charge here?" Wendy wriggled around on the broomstick.

Snowflake sighed and turned the broomstick to the left – straight into a scuffle of squabbling witches.

There was a loud whining noise and the broomstick went into a dive.

Wendy wailed as they headed towards the ground and Snowflake was so scared he thought his fur would turn from black to white. They crashed into a deep, dark,

muddy hole at the side of the road.

"Oops!" gulped Snowflake. "Sorry!"

"It's not your fault," said Wendy. "It's mine. I should send back my witch's licence. I'm hopeless."

"No you're not," said Snowflake.

"Yes I am," said Wendy. "I can't make rude noises like other witches."

"But I can make bad smells," said Snowflake, "especially when I've had a tin of sardines for tea."

"I can't stop frogs croaking," said the witch.

"But you've got a wonderful magic potion for sore throats," said Snowflake.

"And worst of all I can't see because I haven't got a proper hat," she sobbed.

"But you do have a wonderful cat," said Snowflake and he licked her chin.

Witch Wendy climbed out of the hole and sat on the grass verge with her head in her hands. Snowflake scrambled out after her and looked around.

"Can you see what I see?" he asked. "Or has that bump on the head affected my eyes?"

Wendy looked up. She blinked. She jumped to her feet and did a little dance. She gave Snowflake a huge hug. There, at the side of the road was a long row of witch's hats.

Chapter Three

Wendy picked up one of the hats and tried it on.

"What do you think?" she asked Snowflake.

"Well," he replied, "it's not as black as your old hat, and it's not as shiny, and it does have a sort of bobble on the top, but apart from that it's purrfect."

"I'll have it," giggled Wendy. "What a bit of luck." Suddenly she looked serious. "You don't think all these hats belong to somebody do you, Snowflake?"

"No," said Snowflake shaking his head, "they probably fell off the back of a broomstick."

"In that case," said the witch, "I might as well take all of them. It's always useful to have a few spare hats."

She gathered up all the hats, stacked them one on top of the other and balanced them on her head.

They hauled the slimy broomstick out of the deep hole and climbed aboard.

"Wait a minute," said Wendy just as Snowflake was ready to take off.

She hopped off the broomstick and hooked her old hat out of the hole with her wand. She placed it carefully at the side of the road.

"There," she said, looking very pleased with herself. "I think that looks just right."

Wendy climbed into bed just as dawn was breaking.

"I can't wait to see what Rosemary is going to say about my new hat," she giggled. "It's so unusual with that bobble on the top. Don't you think she'll be jealous, Snowflake?"

Snowflake snuggled down in his basket and closed his eyes.

"I think she'll be spellbound," he murmured.

Chapter Four

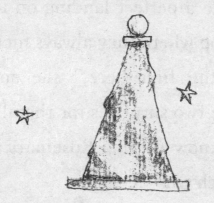

The next night was a full moon. For once Wendy couldn't wait to set off for Saturday night flying practice.

She sat up straight and tall in her new hat and enjoyed watching the twinkling stars and the feel of the cool air as it stroked her face. The broomstick didn't bump or jolt or stall once. She felt like a new witch.

She made a perfect landing on top of the bus stop where they always met.

"We're the first here," she smiled. "That'll be two surprises for them!"

"I don't know whether Rosemary is the sort of witch who likes surprises," said Snowflake.

Wendy straightened the hat on her head as Rosemary, Harriet and Primrose whizzed into view. The three witches braked suddenly and skidded into one another in front of the bus stop. Witch Rosemary scanned Wendy from top to toe.

"Where did you get that hat?" she screeched. Her green skin turned violet in the moonlight and her yellow eyes glowed red at the rims.

"How did you manage that? You can't even make a decent smell let alone a designer hat spell."

"Do you like it?" Wendy smiled.

"I want one!" Rosemary pranced up and down angrily. "Tell me how you did it."

"It's a secret," said Snowflake.

Witch Rosemary screamed like a hyena. Coalface, her cat, spat like a snake. Then Rosemary rummaged in her handbag and got out her purse.

"I'll buy that one off you. However much you want – name your price."

Wendy shook her head.

"This one's mine. But if you really want one . . ."

"I want one too," pleaded Primrose.

"And me," added Harriet.

"Twenty pounds," snarled Rosemary,

waving the money in front of her.

"Each?" queried Snowflake.

Rosemary, Primrose and Harriet nodded so hard their warts wobbled.

"I'm not sure . . ." said Wendy.

"Done," said Snowflake, whisking the money out of the witches' hands. "We'll bring the hats tomorrow night."

Flying practice went like a dream.

Wendy sprinted around church spires. She hurtled over high trees and she didn't tangle with telephone wires once. Rosemary, Primrose and Harriet went home early in a sulk.

But Wendy and Snowflake stayed out

looping the loop until the sun started
to lighten the inky sky.

Later, as they snuggled up on the
sofa, half asleep, Wendy whispered in
Snowflake's ear.

"With a new hat my spells will be—"

"—enchanting," murmured
Snowflake.

"And my broomstick racing will be—"

"—record-breaking," murmured Snowflake.

"And it's all happened like—"

"—like magic?" murmured Snowflake.

"Yes!" said Witch Wendy. "Just like magic."

Chapter Five

Witch Rosemary was very pleased with her new hat. She studied her reflection in a puddle. She smiled, a horrible, crooked smile that showed rows of black and yellow rotting teeth.

"I think it suits me better than you," she said to Wendy.

"I'm glad you like it," said Wendy.

"Oh, I do," snarled Rosemary. "I'm very happy and tonight's witch-hunt in the woods is going to be the best one we've had for ages. We'll catch voles and toads and spiders by the sackful."

"Yippee!" yelled Primrose and Harriet

as they collected their new hats. "That sounds spooky."

"Sounds tasty to me," miaowed Nightshade, Primrose's cat, as he spread flying ointment on Primrose's broomstick.

"Sounds mouth-watering to me," Coalface called, licking his lips.

"Sounds lovely to me," sang Sable,

Witch Harriet's cat. "What do you think, Snowflake?"

Snowflake sighed from the pads of his paws to the ends of his ears. He blushed from the roots of his fur to the tips of his whiskers.

Sable lounged on her purple velvet cushion at the back of Harriet's broomstick and gazed at him with bluebell coloured eyes.

"Lovely," Snowflake replied. But he didn't mean the voles and toads and spiders.

"Hold on to your hats," screamed Rosemary as she rose into the air, spun the broomstick around three times and sped off deep into the countryside.

Snowflake closed his eyes and clung on with all his claws as Wendy darted after her.

The witches were so happy with their new hats they dribbled, burped and sang very badly all the way to the Woeful Wood. It was pitch-black as they whirled amongst the trees collecting bags of beetles, sacks of snails and saucepans full of spiders.

There was a crack of thunder overhead

and a flash of lightning filtered through the trees.

"Here comes the delicious downpour," cackled Rosemary.

Huge drops of water began to splash to the ground.

"On to the pond for a toad hunt!" she cried, pointing the way with a flick of her gnarled fingers.

By the time they reached the edge of the wood the rain was teeming down. Wendy pulled her hat further down over her face and wiped her muddy hands on her cloak. She looked at the mud for a moment, puzzled. Then she looked at Rosemary, Primrose and Harriet.

The rain was washing their new hats clean. As the mud ran over the brims and on to their clothes, the hats changed to red and white, topped with an orange plastic bobble.

"What's happening to our hats?" wailed Harriet.

"Oh dear," gulped Snowflake as Wendy

watched, horrified. "I think it's time to go home. Fast."

Wendy twizzled the broomstick around and scooted for safety.

"Wendy, you wimp of a witch," roared Rosemary as she wiped her muddy hands all over Sable. "Come back here. Come and explain why our new hats have turned into traffic cones!"

Chapter Six

Witch Rosemary was in a rage. She kicked her traffic cone across Wendy's garden and hammered on the front door. Primrose and Harriet rattled at the windows and the three cats caterwauled down the chimney.

"You've gone too far this time," Rosemary screeched.

"It was a mistake," sobbed Wendy through the letter box. "You know I get in a muddle sometimes."

"You're so irritating I should turn you into a wasp," shouted Rosemary.

Snowflake opened the door a crack.

"Can we do a deal?" he asked, waving

three twenty-pound notes under Rosemary's hooked nose. "You'll get your money back if you don't make any mean magic."

Rosemary hissed like the sound of the wind whipping down a long tunnel.

She stretched out an ugly hand, grabbed the money and clambered on to her broomstick.

"You've got off lightly this time, Wendy," she called as she collected Coalface from the roof. Then she jammed Harriet and Primrose's hats over the chimney pot, sending smoke swirling back into the house.

"Oh, Snowflake," coughed Wendy. "I can't go around wearing a traffic cone for a hat. What am I going to do?"

The next night Snowflake took Wendy to look for her old hat. It was very foggy  and they could hardly find their way around.

Finally, they found the right place, but the hole had been filled in and there was no sign of Wendy's old hat. She took the traffic cone off her head and scowled at it.

"I need a proper hat," she wailed. "What sort of a witch doesn't have a hat?"

She threw the cone down in a temper. As it hit the ground, the orange bobble on the top began to flash.

"Brilliant," Snowflake beamed, picking up the cone. "It's a light. It will help us see where we're going." He put it back on Wendy's head.

"What's that noise?" asked Wendy.

"What's that smell?" asked Snowflake.

"WITCHES!" they both said at once.

"Quickly," said Wendy, "I don't want them to see me. Hide in the hedge."

The noises got louder and the smell got stronger.

"Ouch! Eek! Mind your elbows. I can't

see where I'm going. I think we're lost," voices whimpered out of the fog. There were horrible sounds of skidding, splintering wood, head-banging, and then a huge thud right in front of Wendy and Snowflake.

A tangle of witches stared at them. Rosemary crawled out of the pile.

"I can see you, Wendy," she snarled. "There's no point trying to hide when you've got a great big flashing light on top of your head."

"You're just jealous," said Wendy, standing up with her hands on her hips. She adjusted her hat so that the orange beam lit up the sky around them. "Soon, everyone will want one of these hats. They are not only stylish but also perfectly practical for a foul, foggy night."

"See and be seen, that's our motto," Snowflake agreed.

He settled down on the back of the broomstick as Wendy climbed on the front.

"It'll take you hours to find your way home in this weather," said Wendy, "so

I wouldn't lie around here if I were you."

Rosemary, Primrose and Harriet were stunned into silence.

Wendy and Snowflake soared skywards, laughing so much that the broomstick rocked backwards and forwards like a see-saw.

Very early next morning a huddle of bruised witches and bandaged cats arrived at Wendy's house.

"Have you still got those lovely red-and-white hats?" called Rosemary.

"Perhaps," replied Snowflake through the keyhole. "Why?"

"We feel it's time for a change," said Harriet.

"Black's a bit boring," said Primrose.

"We'll pay you double," said Rosemary.

"Sold," said Snowflake, whizzing out of the front door and snatching the money. "They're perfect for moonless nights and winter weather. Don't you agree?"

Later, Wendy sat polishing her hat in front of the fire.

"There are a couple of things I don't understand," she said.

"What?" asked Snowflake.

"Firstly, why is our kitchen overflowing with ice-cream cones?"

"They were on special offer," fibbed Snowflake. This was the first time he'd had a go at a spell all on his own. He thought the odd mistake was understandable.

"Don't you think they would make good hats for cats?" mused Wendy.

"Oh, no!" growled Snowflake. "Categorically not. What's the other thing you don't understand?"

"Why did Rosemary, Primrose and Harriet come here for the traffic cones?" asked Wendy. "Why didn't they

get them from the side of the road?
There must be plenty of them around."

Snowflake rolled his eyes up to the
ceiling and leaned hard against the
dining room door to try and close it. At
the second spelling attempt, Snowflake

had got it right. He'd charmed all the traffic cones in the neighbourhood straight into Wendy's dining room.

"There's something I've been meaning to tell you," Snowflake purred.

But Wendy wasn't listening. She pulled on her hat, switched on the flashing light and waltzed around the room waving her wand.

"Snowflake," she asked, "do you think Rosemary will be a bit nicer to me now?"

"I'm afraid that," giggled Snowflake, "is just witchful thinking!"

Broom Broom!

For my mother

Chapter One

Witch Wendy couldn't believe it, her broomstick had broken down! Wendy tried everything: she chanted all the broomstick breakdown spells in the book; she soaked it in flying ointment; and finally, she whacked it with her wand. Nothing worked. The broomstick was kaput!

"What am I going to do?" she wailed at Snowflake, her cat. "The Broomstick Race is only two nights away and I haven't got anything to fly on!"

Snowflake sighed. He handed Wendy her hat and picked up the broken broomstick.

"We'll just have to go to the garage to get it mended," he said.

"But how will we get there?" asked Wendy.

"Walk, of course," replied Snowflake.

"Witches aren't *meant* to walk," Wendy scowled.

"Cats aren't *meant* to fly," said Snowflake, "but every night I'm catapulted into the sky. Now, are you coming or not?"

Wendy sulked all the way to the Broom Broom Garage while Snowflake pulled the broomstick.

There was a big silver sign above the

garage. It read: *We'll put the Vroom back in your broom.*

"I hope he means that," said Wendy.

Mr Revit, the repair man, looked at the broomstick and pursed his lips.

"Has it been in a crash?" he asked.

"One or two," murmured Snowflake.

"Nothing major." Wendy smiled her most bewitching smile. "Just the odd little prang."

Mr Revit didn't look convinced.

"It'll take a week," he said.

"A week!" Wendy shrieked. "I haven't got a week. The Witches' Annual Broomstick Race is on Midsummer's Eve. That's the night after tomorrow!"

"We'll have to buy another broomstick," said Snowflake.

Mr Revit shook his head.

"It's been worse than Halloween in here for the last couple of days. I haven't got any broomsticks left."

"Well, that's it then," said Wendy as they walked home. "I can't take part in the Broomstick Race."

"Look on the bright side," said Snowflake,

secretly quite pleased. "At least we won't come last again."

"But we'll have to sit with the elves and the fairies and the weak and wimpy witches," whined Wendy. "Then there's Rosemary, Primrose and Harriet. You know what they'll say."

"What?" yawned Snowflake.

"If you don't take part in the broomstick race, it's a whole year until you can show your face."

"So we wouldn't be able to go out for a year?" Snowflake asked.

"Only on our own," said Wendy. "But we wouldn't be allowed to mix with other witches – or their cats."

Snowflake pulled his whiskers and twanged them back into place. He thought of Witch Harriet's cat, Sable, and he felt his legs go all wobbly. Then he thought of Witch Rosemary's cat, Coalface. Coalface would have a whole year to use his charms on Sable.

Snowflake suddenly
made up his mind.

"Of course you must
take part in the race,"
he said.

"But how?" asked Wendy.

"Witches don't have to use broomsticks,
do they?" asked Snowflake.

"Well, no," said Wendy.

"Witches sometimes use other forms of
transport, don't they?" asked Snowflake.

"Well, yes," said Wendy.

"Then we'll find something else to fly
on," said Snowflake.

Witch Wendy picked Snowflake up and

kissed the top of his head.

"Snowflake," she said. "I'm so lucky to have you. I know you always have my best interests at heart."

Chapter Two

Wendy and Snowflake had nearly reached home when they saw three shadowy shapes hurtling through the sky.

"Watch out, witches about!" warned Snowflake.

Wendy hurried up the garden path. Something smelly and scary swooped down and landed in front of her.

"Rosemary!" Wendy took a step backwards. "You startled me!"

"Hee! Hee! Hee!" cackled Rosemary. "That's what witches are meant to do Wendy, or have you forgotten?"

"Hee! Hee! Hee!" echoed Primrose and Harriet, as they hovered over the hedge.

"Of … of course not," stuttered Wendy. "It's just that I don't like scaring people very much."

"Pah!" spat Rosemary. Her eyes narrowed and turned deep pink like slivers of beetroot. "Wendy, why are you a walking witch? Where's your broomstick?"

"It's … it's giving me a bit of bother," Wendy stammered.

"Are you going to miss the Broomstick Race?" Rosemary leered and pushed her beaky nose close to Wendy's face. "What a pity."

"An absolute cat-astrophe," crowed Coalface.

Snowflake arched his back and swished his tail.

"I don't suppose anyone's got a spare broomstick?" Wendy asked.

"Well—" began Harriet.

"Borrowing broomsticks is against the Flyway Code," Rosemary ranted. "You'll just have to sit on the skyline, Wendy, with the other wimpy witches."

"Oh no, she won't," growled Snowflake. "It's all sorted out. I've found a replacement broomstick."

"What?" exclaimed Rosemary, Primrose and Harriet.

"What?" whispered Wendy.

"Really?" sneered Rosemary. "I expect it's a garden spade or a mop? They don't fly at all well. It'll take you a year to finish the race!"

Her horrible cackle made the moon quiver and the stars shrink into the night sky.

"It's neither of those," said Snowflake.

"Tell me what it is," Rosemary roared. "I want to know."

"You'll have to wait and see," said Snowflake. "But it's even better than a broomstick."

"Better than a broomstick?" cackled Primrose and Harriet, almost falling into the hedge they laughed so much.

"I'm so-o-o-o scared," sneered Rosemary. "Positively squirming on my seat!"

"Cowering in our cloaks!" agreed Primrose.

"Fretting from our foreheads to our feet!" sang Harriet.

"And so you should be!" shouted Snowflake, as he dragged Wendy into the house. "You should be three worried witches," and he slammed the front door shut.

Chapter Three

"So," whispered Wendy as soon as the witches were out of eavesdropping distance, "what is it then?"

"What's what?" asked Snowflake, putting down his toothbrush and climbing into his basket.

"What is it that's even better than a

broomstick?" Wendy sighed.

"Oh, that," yawned Snowflake. "I don't know yet, but we'll think of something."

"Well?" asked Wendy after breakfast the next evening. "Have you thought of something?"

"I'm working on it," said Snowflake. "You can't rush a genius. Have you noticed all these cobwebs around the ceiling?"

"Witches' houses are meant to be full of cobwebs," murmured Wendy.

"They make me sneeze," said Snowflake.

He prised open a cupboard door with his paw and took out some cleaning materials.

"That's it!" shouted Wendy, jumping up, spilling her tea and tossing her toast and marmalade into the air. "You are a genius, Snowflake!"

"I am?" queried Snowflake.

Wendy skipped to the cupboard.

"This is what we'll use: a feather duster.

It's the right shape, it's light and it'll glide through the air like …"

"… like a bird breaking the speed limit," grinned Snowflake.

"Let's try it out," said Wendy, rubbing some flying ointment along the handle. "Hop on the back."

Snowflake rushed to get his crash helmet and settled on the pink, yellow and blue feathers. He tried to get comfortable while Wendy concocted a spell.

"Feather duster, rise to the ceiling,

Flap your tail

and send the cobwebs reeling."

The feather duster rose slowly into the air and glided around the room, flicking at the cobwebs.

Snowflake started to giggle. He started to wiggle. The feather duster started to wobble.

"Sit still," commanded Wendy.

"I can't help it," Snowflake gasped.

The feather duster rocked violently from side to side. It reared up like a horse and then charged headlong into the fireplace.

Wendy was covered in soot and Snowflake had a splinter up his nose.

"Sorry," Snowflake sniffed. "I don't think that will work."

"Not if you don't sit still," snapped Wendy.

"I couldn't. The feathers were tickling my bottom," said Snowflake.

"We'll just have to think of something else," said Wendy.

Snowflake scraped the marmalade and toast off the rug and put it in the bin.

"It's a bit obvious," he said, "but I don't suppose you've considered a flying carpet?"

"We could try it, I suppose," said Wendy, whipping the rug out from underneath the table. "We'll take it outside, where there's more room."

Wendy put the rug in the middle of the lawn and sat down on it.

Snowflake stood at the back and dug his

claws into the carpet.

"Carpet, rise into the air,

And up to the clouds if you dare!"

Nothing happened. Wendy tapped it with her wand. She put a blob of flying ointment at each corner. She tried again.

"Carpet, rise above the ground,

Or in the dustbin you'll be found!"

The rug rose a few inches above the grass and hovered.

"O-o-o-h!" wailed Snowflake as the carpet crumpled and crinkled in the middle. "I'm going to fall off!"

"Nonsense," said Wendy. "It's just a question of getting used to it, that's all."

"Carpet, head for the nearest tree,
Let's see how quick you
can really be!"

The rug jerked towards a large oak tree.

It was heading straight for the tree trunk.

"Help!" wailed Snowflake.

"Stop!" Wendy commanded the carpet.

The carpet didn't take any notice.

"Jump!" shouted Snowflake.

Wendy and Snowflake jumped and sploshed straight into the garden pond. The carpet crashed into the tree and slid to the ground like a stunned snake.

"It's hopeless!" Wendy spluttered. "We can't take part in the broomstick race unless one of us has a marvellous, magical idea."

Chapter Four

It was Midsummer's Eve. The weather was perfect for broomstick racing. The sky was as clear as a crystal ball, with a helpful breeze to blow them along – but Wendy was glum. She hadn't found anything suitable to fly on.

"Cooo-eee," a witchy voice called down Wendy's chimney.

"What do you want, Rosemary?" Wendy sighed.

"Are you ready for the Broomstick Race?" asked Rosemary in her sneakiest, meanest voice.

"She knows I'm not," Wendy said to Snowflake. "She just wants to gloat."

Snowflake raced over to the windows and pulled the curtains across as Primrose and Harriet pressed their warty noses against the glass.

He just caught a glimpse of Sable's glossy fur and green eyes. She looked beautiful in the moonlight.

"See you next year, dear," cackled

Rosemary. She circled the chimney pot and blew down it so hard that Wendy's fire went out.

"We'll see you sooner than that, or I'm not a cat, *dear*," Snowflake wheezed up the chimney.

"Piffle!" Rosemary spat, and the three witches flew off in a frantic flurry.

"Who needs a fire extinguisher with Rosemary around?" Wendy coughed through clouds of smoke.

Suddenly Snowflake flung his paws around her and licked her face.

"You're a wonder-witch! Put your racing clothes on. Hurry, or we'll be late."

"Hold on, Snowflake," Wendy sobbed, "there's a small problem. We haven't got anything to ride on."

Snowflake whipped the bright red fire extinguisher off the wall.

"We have now," he said. "Just think of this as a supersonic broomstick. Rosemary will be mean with envy. Trust me."

Snowflake checked his watch. The race was due to start at midnight – they had ten minutes to get there.

Wendy put on her traffic-cone hat, turned on the light and sat at the front of the fire extinguisher.

"Let's have a spell," said Snowflake.

"I don't know any fire-extinguisher spells," said Wendy.

"Make one up then," said Snowflake.

"Something like:

    Fire extinguisher travel into the night,

    Take us to the race with all your might."

Snowflake rubbed the flying ointment on the metal container.

Wendy tapped it three times with her wand.

The extinguisher rumbled inside, it juddered, then it rose into the air and hovered for a moment in the doorway.

"It's not going to work," said Wendy.

"It's just warming up, that's all," said Snowflake.

As soon as he said this, the extinguisher began to taxi down the garden path. Then it thundered up the road and launched itself towards the clouds.

They were at the race in eight minutes. Everyone was lined up at the starting star. Wendy edged in next to Rosemary.

"What on earth … ?"

The waiting witches stared at the supersonic broomstick.

"You can't be serious," hooted Harriet.

"It's so embarrassing," bawled Primrose.

"It must be against the rules," hissed Rosemary.

The Chief Wizard came over. He inspected the supersonic broomstick very carefully.

Wendy could hardly breathe. If she was disqualified here, in front of everyone, she would never, ever be able to show her face again.

The wizard stroked his beard and muttered to himself under his moustache. Snowflake looked at the starting star and made a wish. Then he nuzzled his nose against Wendy's back.

The wizard shook his head several times. It wasn't a good omen.

Chapter Five

"There's nothing in the rule book to say it isn't allowed," mused the wizened wizard.

"Well, there should be," snapped Rosemary. "I shall re-write the book for next year."

"You may take part," said the wizard to

Wendy. He bowed deeply.

"Yes-s-s!" said Wendy and Snowflake, clasping hand and paw together.

"It's disgraceful," spluttered Primrose.

"Such a let down," Harriet jeered.

"I expect you'll come last again," snarled Rosemary, pushing to the front with her superb stick. "It's not exactly streamlined, is it?"

"As long as I finish the race, I don't mind," said Wendy.

"Pah!" spat Rosemary. "Everyone wants to win."

Wendy shrank back into the swarm of witches and waited for the wizard to light the Fantastic Firework to start the race.

"Ready, witches," warned the wizard. "Steady, cats, GO!"

The firework soared into space and exploded in a torrent of tiny orange sparks.

Rosemary got off to a flying start, launching herself towards the ground. The sparks rained down on to her cloak like a sprinkling of glitter. The witches nosedived after her.

Wendy and Snowflake whizzed over woods, swept across streams and raced along empty roads. For once there weren't any mishaps. Wendy felt wonderful.

Even Snowflake was quite enjoying himself.

"Only one more lap to go," he called, after they'd been around the course six times.

Rosemary was out in front, whipping her broomstick with her wand. She was travelling so fast that she seemed to glow in the dark.

Wendy leaned forwards and whispered into the wind.

"Fire extinguisher,
we need to be quick,
Just like a
supersonic broomstick!"

"Mia-ow," cried Snowflake as the fire extinguisher lurched away from the other witches.

It sped past Primrose and Harriet and skimmed through the sky towards Rosemary.

Wendy and Snowflake pulled up alongside. Rosemary was furious.

"Go away," she screeched. "You shouldn't be up here. You must be cheating."

"I told you to watch out," said Snowflake. He sniffed the air. He could smell burning. Little plumes of smoke spiralled out from under Rosemary's cloak. The broomstick was making a crackling, crunching noise.

"You'd better slow down, Rosemary!" called Snowflake. "Your broomstick's over-heating."

"Nonsense," stormed Rosemary. "I'm not going to fall for any of your cat tricks."

"We're nearly there!" Wendy called excitedly to Snowflake. "I can see the

Finishing Well. There are two frogs either side of it waving flags. It's just the other side of those trees."

The other witches were catching up. They whooped and yelled and pointed with their gnarled fingers.

"Fire!" they shrieked. "Rosemary's on fire!"

Snowflake looked at the back of Rosemary's broomstick. Flames were starting to unfurl around the bottom of her cloak.

Coalface was flapping at the flames with his paws.

"Stop!" he mewed at Rosemary. "My bottom's getting hot!"

"Not until we've won," snapped Rosemary.

As they dived in amongst the trees Wendy took the lead. Rosemary was hot on her tail. She bumped the back of the fire extinguisher.

"Let me through, Wendy!"

Wendy zig-zagged from side to side. She weaved up and down.

Rosemary couldn't get past. She gave one last huge thump into the back of Wendy's supersonic broomstick. Wendy lurched forwards and clung to the handle at the front of the fire extinguisher.

Snowflake thudded into her back.

There was a rumbling from inside the extinguisher. It shuddered. It juddered. It felt as if it was going to explode. A jet of foam shot out from the hose at the side and streamed backwards through the air.

It splooshed all over Rosemary and Coalface.

"This is cheating," spluttered Rosemary, trying to see where she was going.

But Wendy didn't hear. She was trying to control the supersonic broomstick. It rolled to the right. Then it lurched to the left.

Wendy and Snowflake slid and slithered on the foam-splattered seat.

Branches battered against Wendy's hat. Twigs tugged at Snowflake's tail.

"We're going to crash," Wendy shouted. "Jump!"

"Here we go again," sighed Snowflake.

Chapter Six

Wendy was buried under some brambles. Snowflake spotted the flashing light on top of her hat.

"Out you come," he said pulling the prickly stems away with his paws.

"Oh, Snowflake," Wendy sobbed. "We'd so nearly won the race. Now we'll have come last again. I can't bear it!"

"Never mind," said Snowflake. "It's the taking part that counts."

Wendy hauled herself up. She was covered in scratches, her flying cloak was torn to shreds and she'd lost one of her favourite red shoes.

In the distance Wendy and Snowflake heard clapping and cackling.

"Let's go home," said Snowflake.

"We've got to finish the race," said Wendy. "Those are the rules. I know they'll all laugh, but Rosemary will never let me forget if I don't even get to the Finishing Well."

Snowflake thought of Rosemary covered in foam. He sniggered.

Then he thought how cross she would be and he shivered.

"Are you sure?" said Snowflake. He looked at his messy coat. "Think of all the catty remarks I'll get from Coalface and Sable and Nightshade when they see me looking like this."

But Wendy wasn't listening. She was already picking her way through the undergrowth in the direction of the witches' whooping.

Snowflake tried to tidy himself up with a quick lick and then he followed her out of the trees towards the other witches.

Two foamy figures stood by the Finishing Well. The Chief Wizard handed over the winner's cauldron to the one with the pointy hat.

Suddenly, the watching witches were eerily silent.

"Is that Rosemary?" Wendy asked Snowflake.

"I'm afraid so," said Snowflake.

"What happened to her? Oh, dear, it wasn't anything to do with us, was it?"

"I was going to mention that," Snowflake fidgeted.

"She looks furious," whispered Wendy.

Underneath the white foam Rosemary's skin glowed a livid green. Her eyes blazed red and her tongue darted in and out like a lizard.

"Wendy!" Rosemary growled, spitting foam everywhere. "Come here!"

Wendy tiptoed towards Rosemary.

"I don't know what to say," she started. "You are the most in … in …"

"… incredible?" prompted Snowflake.

"No!" raged Rosemary.

"… intelligent?" said Snowflake helpfully.

"NO!" screamed Rosemary, hurling the cauldron to the ground.

"you are absolutely in ..."

"... ingenious," said the Chief Wizard. "That is what I think our winner is trying to say. Am I right?"

Rosemary froze.

She made a whistling noise like a kettle coming to the boil, and then she nodded.

It was a very tiny nod but everyone saw it.

"Ingenious?" Wendy gasped. "Me?"

"You lost the race so you could save Rosemary and Coalface," said Harriet.

"*So* generous," purred Sable.

"I did?" said Wendy.

"You did," said Snowflakc, nipping the back of her leg.

"If you hadn't been flying that fire extinguisher, I dread to think what would have happened," said Primrose.

"The sparks from the starting firework landed in Rosemary's cloak and began to smoulder ..." Harriet said.

"... until they burst into fierce flames," continued Primrose.

"... and singed my whiskers," interrupted Coalface. "I've lost all my looks."

"Three chants for Wendy!" praised the witches.

"A cluster of catcalls for Snowflake!" called Sable.

"And I think Rosemary has something to give you," said Harriet, "to show how grateful she is."

Rosemary scowled.

She stamped her foot.

She pouted her lips.

Then she pushed the winner's cauldron

into Wendy's arms.

"Oh, I can't accept this," said Wendy.

"Yes, you can," said Snowflake. "We'll scratch your name here underneath Rosemary's. By the way," he flashed his eyes at Sable, "I don't suppose anyone can offer us a lift home?"

Later, Snowflake lay in his basket dreaming
of Sable. Wendy danced around the room
clutching the winner's cauldron.

"Snowflake," she said, "can I ask you
something?"

"Fire away," said Snowflake, lazily opening one eye.

"Do you think Rosemary will be a bit nicer to me because I stopped her going up in smoke?"

"Now that," giggled Snowflake, "is the burning question!"

Cat
Tricks

For Brenda

Chapter One

Witch Wendy was in a flap. She was late for the weekly witches' meeting again and her broomstick refused to go any faster.

"Witch Rosemary is so cross if we're not on time," Wendy moaned. "She's bound to cast a spiteful spell on me."

Snowflake, her cat, clung to the back of the broomstick. He was all of a quiver.

"Coalface is so catty when we're late," he groaned. "He's bound to sharpen his claws on me."

The broomstick crashed into the kerb and screeched to a stop outside

the Hairy Wart pub. There was a dreadful din coming from inside. It was the sound of whooping wizards and wittering witches.

Wendy gave Snowflake a little pat. Snowflake rubbed his cheek along the side of Wendy's shoe. They sidled into the Cock's Tail Bar together.

"We're not too late, are we?" Wendy whispered to Snowflake. "Rosemary won't be too mean . . . will she?"

"She looks in a t-terrible t-temper to me," Snowflake stuttered. "And Coalface looks like a real sour puss."

Snowflake pointed to the dingiest, darkest corner where a horrible

 hunched-up figure squatted on a stool. On her lap was a furious-faced cat. Wendy trembled from the point of her hat down to the tips of her toenails.

"Oh dear," she said. "Wait for the snarling."

"And the spitting," Snowflake frowned.

"And the scratching," Wendy quaked.

"And that's just Rosemary," Snowflake sighed.

Wendy jumped as someone yanked

at her hair. "Ouch!" she shrieked, spinning around.

Witch Harriet and Witch Primrose stood behind her.

"Here you are at last," tut-tutted Primrose.

"Rosemary wouldn't wait," Harriet sniffed. "We had the Magic Meeting without you."

"Did I miss anything important?" Wendy murmured.

Primrose and Harriet looked at each other. They gulped. They sniggered. Then they jutted out their hairy chins and laughed and laughed.

"What's the matter with *them*?" Wendy asked Snowflake.

"More importantly," Snowflake whispered, "what's the matter with Rosemary?"

Witch Rosemary sat silently in the corner.

"No roaring with rage," Wendy said.

"No hateful hissing," Snowflake added, feeling anxious.

"In fact," Wendy murmured, "it's . . ."

". . . scary," they both said together.

Wendy decided to be brave. She straightened her traffic cone hat, stretched her short body as tall as it would go and walked up to the warty old witch.

"Are you all right, Rosemary?" Wendy asked.

Rosemary twitched and lifted her head. She pulled a horrible face, stuck out a furry tongue and gave a faint gurgle.

Wendy peered at her. Her skin was grisly green and her eyes glowed sickly yellow as usual, but she didn't seem herself. Primrose and Harriet both looked sad.

"Poor Rosemary," Primrose sniffled.

"It's the most terrible news," Harriet gulped.

"She's lost her cackle," Primrose cried. "It wafted away on the West wind and didn't come back."

Snowflake started to smile. Wendy tried hard not to laugh.

"So," Wendy said, "Rosemary can't talk?"

Primrose and Harriet shook their heads and each shed three tears.

"It's a tragedy," Harriet wailed. "Rosemary is completely and utterly screechless!"

Chapter Two

"Are you still a scaredy cat?" Wendy asked Snowflake.

He shook his head.

"Are you still a twitchy witch?" Snowflake asked Wendy.

She shook her head.

"There won't be any mean magic

from Rosemary tonight," Snowflake sniggered. "We can relax."

Harriet's cat, Sable, was curled up in front of the fire. Snowflake strolled up to her. "That colour fur really suits you, Sable," he gushed. "You should wear it more often."

"I think I'm going to be sick," said Primrose's cat, Nightshade.

Snowflake ignored him. Sable smiled. Snowflake felt his legs wobble.

"You seem very cheerful," she purred, "considering."

Snowflake stared into her beautiful blue eyes. "Considering what?" he asked dreamily.

"You obviously haven't heard the news," Nightshade smirked.

"Rosemary has to go into hospital, so Coalface is coming to stay."

Snowflake admired the way Sable's whiskers fanned out neatly.

"Poor you," murmured Snowflake.

"You just don't understand, do you?" Sable sang in her velvety voice. "The witches took a vote before you arrived. Coalface is coming to stay with *you*!"

As soon as they got home Snowflake went straight to bed.

"My life is ruined," he moaned, "for ever and ever!"

"Nonsense," Wendy said. "It's only for a few nights while Rosemary goes to the Cackle Clinic to get a new screech. Perhaps Coalface isn't so bad once you get to know him properly."

"Perhaps dogs don't bark and the night isn't dark," Snowflake sobbed.

"Of course he's bad! He fights and he bites and he's always making catty comments!"

"Well, we've just got to make the best of it," said Wendy. "Now try and get some rest. He'll be here first thing in the evening."

"I shall have daymares," Snowflake snuffled. "I won't sleep properly. I shall have to take cat naps when he's not around."

"Snowflake," Wendy said, snuggling down in her bed. "It's for three nights. How bad can it be?"

"It won't just be bad," muttered Snowflake. "It'll be the pits."

Chapter Three

Snowflake woke up with a start. An amber eye glinted at the keyhole and heavy breathing slithered through the letter box.

"Oi, fishbreath," someone grunted. "Let me in."

"You're too early," said Snowflake.

"It's barely dark."

"I'm cold and I'm wet and I'm very hungry," Coalface grunted. "Now let me in or I'll caterwaul loudly enough to wake all the witches in the world."

Snowflake opened the door and Coalface strolled in. He glanced around the room. Wendy was still snoring soundly in her bed.

"This isn't like a witch's house at all." Coalface wrinkled up his nose. "It's clean and tidy, and it smells disgusting."

"That's Herbfresh furniture polish," Snowflake said.

"But where are the spiders and the piles of mouse droppings? Where is the cauldron full of gunge and the slime running down the walls? Where is the *mess*?" Coalface growled.

Wendy woke up and jumped out of bed. "Coalface! How . . . lovely to see you. Has Snowflake got you any breakfast?"

"Fish is my favourite," Coalface smirked.

"Since when?" Snowflake whispered.

"Since a second ago," he chuckled, sharpening his claws on the table leg.

Snowflake buried his face in his paws as Wendy opened the cupboard and took out his special tin of pilchards. She gave it all to Coalface. Then she went into the kitchen and came back with his best bowl, full of cream. She gave that to Coalface too.

Snowflake scowled and gave a tiny growl.

"We must make him feel welcome," Wendy whispered, "or he might turn nasty."

"Yummy," murmured Coalface as he

crunched the
pilchards. Then
he spat the
bones out on
to the carpet.

"Scrummy," gurgled Coalface as he
lapped up the cream. Then he wiped
his mouth on the tablecloth and
burped. "Perhaps it's not so bad here
after all," he scowled.

Coalface padded over to Snowflake's
basket. He got in it. Snowflake stared
at Wendy. He glared at Wendy. She
gave him a sorry smile. Coalface
yawned loudly.

"It's been so quiet since Rosemary

lost her cackle," he said. "I'm quite worn out!" He closed his eyes and went to sleep.

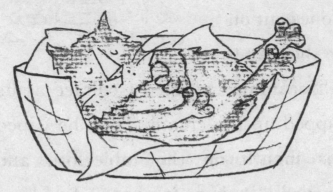

"Well," said Wendy happily, "he seems to have made himself at home." She picked up her wand from the table and skipped across the room. She paused in front of a pale-pink door with a silver handle in the shape of a star.

"While Coalface is resting, I'll make some potions in my Pink Pantry."

"Can you find something to make him disappear?" Snowflake called, but Wendy had already slipped through the door and closed it firmly behind her.

Snowflake swept up the fish bones, put the tablecloth in the washing machine and fitted a big padlock to the fish cupboard. Snowflake heard a tap at the window. He looked up. Nightshade and Sable pressed their noses to the glass.

"Has he arrived?" Sable asked.

"Has he been bad?" asked Nightshade.

"He's eaten all my prize pilchards, finished off the cream, and he's sleeping in my basket," replied Snowflake. "And he's got disgusting table manners."

"Oh dear," murmured Sable. "You're such a hero to put up with him."

"Do you think so?" Snowflake perked up. He smiled his most charming smile. "Well, if Coalface gets too troublesome I'll just get rid of him."

"You wouldn't dare!" Sable cried.

"I would," bluffed Snowflake. "I'm not the cowardly cat you seem to think I am."

"Hmph," said Nightshade. "I think you're all growls and no bite. But don't send him to us if you do throw him out."

"But he hasn't done anything really terrible, has he?" Sable asked.

"No," Snowflake replied and a shiver ran up his spine, "not yet."

Chapter Four

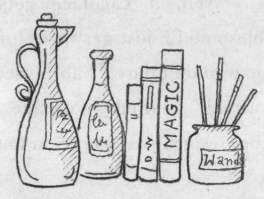

"I've just got to nip out," Wendy said the next night. "It's against the Flyway Code to take two cats on a broomstick so you'll have to stay here."

"Don't worry," Coalface smiled. "I'll make sure Snowball behaves himself."

Snowflake winced. He knew for sure there was trouble ahead.

As soon as Wendy had gone Coalface stretched, flexed his claws and padded towards Snowflake.

"Let's have some fun," he smirked.

"Do . . . do we have to?" Snowflake stammered.

Coalface leaned against the door to Wendy's pantry.

"You can't go in there," said Snowflake.

"Why not?" Coalface rattled the door handle.

"Cats aren't allowed in witches' pantries on their own."

"I can go anywhere I like," said Coalface with a gruesome grin.

He pushed the door open. "It's not even locked," he purred. "Wendy must be a witless witch to be so trusting."

Along the walls of the Pink Pantry were dozens of pearly pink bottles. Each one had a pretty label stuck to the front of it.

"This isn't a proper witch's pantry," Coalface sneered. "Look at all these things: hugging humbugs, caring crystals, rosy raindrops. Pah! Where are the ponging pills and the dreadful dandruff and the beetle blood?"

"We've got mouth-watering mice," Snowflake bristled, "or—"

"Witch Wendy's Simple Spells," Coalface chuckled, picking up a battered book from the table.

"You can't touch that," said Snowflake as Coalface opened the book.

"I can't read what it says." Coalface squinted at the words. "She's got terrible handwriting. Does this say mouse or house?"

"I don't do spells," Snowflake said. He started to feel sick.

"Witch Rosemary often trusts me to do her spells," Coalface boasted. "There is a certain way to do it, of course, and you have to be a special sort of cat. Stylish, handsome, CLEVER."

He looked down his scabby nose at Snowflake. "Perhaps that's why you've never been allowed to make magic. I'll show you how it's done."

"You needn't bother," Snowflake said.

"I'm not leaving this room until I've stirred up a spell," Coalface growled, leafing through the book. "What about Pong of Skunks?"

Snowflake wrinkled up his nose and peeked over Coalface's shoulder.

"Are you sure that doesn't say Song of Monks?"

Coalface hissed and turned the page. "Well, what about Glowering Gloom? That sounds fun."

"Mmm," said Snowflake, "except it could say Flowers in Bloom."

"Yuk!" Coalface grizzled.

"What about this small spell," Snowflake said, "for a blue bottle?"

"Boring!" Coalface yawned.

"But at least we can read it. And Wendy will be back soon."

"All right, Snowy," Coalface snapped.

"Get me a wand."

He took a pink bottle off the shelf and put it on the table.

Snowflake grabbed the nearest wand. It had a label attached to it.

"A Willing Wand," Coalface read, sneering. "How sweet."

"Oh!" Snowflake said. "Are you sure the label says willing?"

"Purrfectly sure." Coalface grinned.

He whisked the wand through the air. He jerked it forwards, he jolted it backwards. Sparks sprinkled out of the wand and smoke swirled around the room. He pointed the wand at the pretty pink bottle.

"With a waving wand at full throttle,
Be transformed into a bluebottle!"

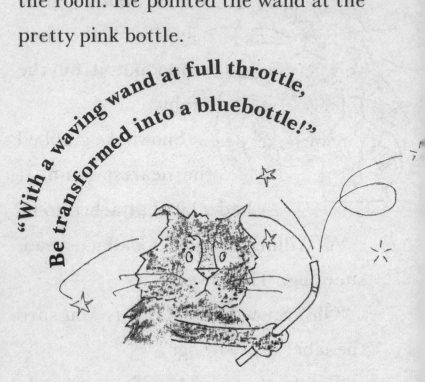

As Coalface chanted the last two words of the spell, the wand wobbled wildly before wilting backwards and pointing straight at Coalface.

Snowflake shielded his eyes as a blaze of light dazzled the room. Then there was a mournful M-I-A-O-WWWWW, followed by an odd hush.

Snowflake peeped out from behind his paws. The wand lay on the floor and the pink bottle still sat on the table – but Coalface had completely vanished.

Chapter Five

"SNOWFLAKE! What are you doing?" Wendy stood in the doorway. "You know this room is out of bounds."

"I was . . . er . . . chasing some mice," said Snowflake, and he hustled a couple of invisible mice back into their holes.

"Where's Coalface?" Wendy frowned.

"He . . ." Snowflake stammered. "He seems to have disappeared."

"Did he say where he was going?" Wendy asked.

Snowflake shook his head. "He was here one minute and gone the next."

"Snowflake, can I smell a spell?" Wendy's nose twitched.

"Categorically not," Snowflake lied.

Wendy walked over to the table and picked up the wand.

"I hope you haven't been using the Wilting Wand. It

could create all sorts of trouble."

She closed up the *Simple Spell Book*. A fly flew up from the page and landed on her hat. She swatted it away. The fly began to buzz. Snowflake ducked as a streak of blue dive-bombed him.

"I've got some good news for you," Wendy said. "Rosemary is coming out

of the Cackle Clinic a night early. She'll be here to collect Coalface tomorrow evening."

The fly circled Snowflake's head, giving an extra loud buzz as it went past each ear.

Wendy picked up a fly swatter. She twirled it in her hand and whirled it over her head. She eyed up the fly.

"I can't stand flies," muttered Wendy, "but bluebottles are the worst of all."

"Did you say BLUEBOTTLE?"

Snowflake gasped. He put his head in his paws. "Oh my wilting whiskers!"

"Snowflake," Wendy asked, "what's the matter?"

"Now promise you won't fly into a temper," he replied, "but—"

Suddenly there was a rattling at the windows and a shaking of the walls.

"Coo-ee!" a voice squealed through the letterbox. "We've all come for a midnight feast."

"You'll have to tell me later," Wendy said.

She shooed Snowflake out of the pantry and closed the door behind her with a firm click.

Primrose and Harriet skipped into the sitting room.

"We've brought fabulous fleabread," said Primrose.

"And crunchy caterpillar cake," trilled Harriet.

"I've made jumping jellies and silly sundaes," Wendy giggled. "Let's go and guzzle them in the garden."

"*We've* come for a cat chat." Sable winked at Snowflake once the witches had left the room. "We've brought slivers of liver to keep Coalface happy. It's his favourite."

"Where is Ugly Mug?" asked Nightshade.

"He's . . . um . . . just buzzed off somewhere," said Snowflake.

"That's odd," said Nightshade.

"Especially as he knew that I was coming," Sable pouted.

There was a humming noise coming from behind the Pink Pantry door. Snowflake saw the key wobble in the lock. There was a clunk as it fell to the floor. Six cat's eyes swivelled round. Something shot out through the keyhole and nosedived towards Snowflake.

Snowflake grabbed his flying helmet and ran for cover. The fly tickled his tail, it belly flopped on his back and it needled his nostrils.

"That fly doesn't like you," said Sable.

"It hates you almost as much as Coalface does," said Nightshade.

The two cats exchanged glances. Nightshade threw back his head and yowled.

"It wasn't my fault!" Snowflake protested, batting away the fly.

"When you said you'd get rid of him, I didn't think you meant magic," Nightshade gasped.

"It's incredible," murmured Sable. "Snowflake, you really are the cat's whiskers."

Chapter Six

Snowflake chased Coalface into the Pink Pantry and trapped him under a glass.

"Primrose says reversing spells are so difficult to get right," said Nightshade.

"You *do* know how to turn him

back?" Sable asked.

"Of course," Snowflake fibbed.

"Because if you don't," Nightshade murmured, "you know what the *Witch's Cat Handbook* says?"

"What?" Snowflake asked.

"You'll have to become Witch Rosemary's cat," Sable replied.

Snowflake tried to smile bravely but his teeth chattered together. He tried to laugh but the sound got tangled in his throat and instead it came out as a long, high-pitched howl.

He couldn't think of anything worse than living with Witch Rosemary.

*

Primrose and Harriet dashed away with their cats just as dawn was breaking.

"Snowflake," Wendy said sternly, "are you sure Coalface didn't say where he was going?"

"Only that he'd got to fly," Snowflake muttered.

"Well, we've got to find him," Wendy said, "or we're both in big trouble."

While Wendy searched the garden, Snowflake padded into the pantry. He scanned the bookshelves.

There were books on *Riotous Recipes* and *Bewitching Buildings*. There were books on *How to Be a Wonderful Witch* and *Fascinating Flyovers of Our Time*, but not one book on undoing spells.

"What am I going to do?" Wendy wailed through the window. "If Rosemary finds out I've lost Coalface she'll banish my broomstick, she'll steal my spell book and . . ."

Wendy gulped.

Her voice dropped to a whisper

". . . and she'll claim my precious cat."

Snowflake went outside and tugged at Wendy's stripy sock with his teeth.

"Come and get some sleep,"

Snowflake said soothingly. "I'll sort everything out."

Snowflake stayed up all day. He searched everywhere for the book to help him undo Coalface's spell. By witches' wake-up time he still hadn't found it.

"I shall have to tell Wendy what's happened," he moaned to himself.

"She probably won't know where the book is, she probably won't be able to get the right spell, and she'll definitely panic. But it's my only hope."

Snowflake took a deep breath and scrambled up on to Wendy's bed. He prodded Wendy gently with his paw. She let out a shuddering snore and turned over. A creased purple pamphlet lay in the space where she had been lying.

Snowflake picked up the slim booklet and read the title: *A Disenchanting Book*.

"I've got it!" Snowflake mewed softly.

He bounded off the bed and rushed into the Pink Pantry. Coalface stared at him from his glass prison. He buzzed as loudly as a mob of bluebottles.

"Be quiet!" Snowflake snapped. "Unless you want me to turn you into a greenfly."

Coalface stopped buzzing, and Snowflake slowly lifted up the glass.

Coalface's big bluebottle eyes bulged angrily, but he stayed quite still.

Snowflake scrabbled through the pages of the purple pamphlet. He picked up a wand with a shaky paw and started the spell.

"Take unbewitching, charmless lore
Make this fly as it was before."

Coalface buzzed briefly but the spell didn't work.

Suddenly the window panes rattled and a horrible noise filled the air. It was a cackle as loud and creepy as any Snowflake had ever heard.

"Oh, my trembling tail," he said. "Witches!"

Coalface buzzed again. He edged backwards across the table.

"Will you stay still?" Snowflake pleaded.

He batted Coalface with his paw. The bluebottle slid into the middle of the table.

Three heavy thuds shook the room and there was a scraping, sliding sound as several tiles slid from the roof and clattered past the window.

They were swiftly followed by three tumbling witches.

"Wendeeeeeeee! It's meeeeeeee!"

Rosemary's voice was as out of tune as ever. Her cackle was crazier and more fur-raising than before.

Snowflake's tail trembled and his legs wobbled. Coalface buzzed backwards, thudding his six bluebottle legs down on the table top.

Snowflake stared at him.

"I wonder," he murmured. "Perhaps if I try the spell backwards."

"Beforewasitasflythismake lorecharmlessunbewitchingtake."

Snowflake couldn't get the words out of his mouth fast enough.

The wand stuttered, it sputtered and Coalface started to spin. As he twizzled he got bigger and bluer and buzzier.

Snowflake closed his eyes.

There was one last huge buzz followed by a gigantic growl.

Snowflake opened one eye. Standing in the middle of the table was Coalface the cat. He looked even bigger and meaner than before. He wiggled his furry bottom, he flattened his tattered

ears and he got ready to pounce.

"Now, Coalface." Snowflake smiled weakly. "Don't be too cross. It was you who insisted on showing me how to do a cat spell."

Coalface hissed and edged forwards. Snowflake inched backwards and tried to pull the pantry door open with his back foot.

"You really wouldn't want me to tell everyone that you're not such a clever cat after all, would you?" Snowflake said in a shaky voice.

"Where is he, then?" Rosemary ranted through all the rooms. "Wendy! Where's my moth-eaten moggie?"

Rosemary pushed past Wendy, Primrose and Harriet and marched into the Pink Pantry.

"Rosemary," Wendy ran after her, "I've got something to tell you. I'm so sorry . . . Coalface is missing."

"What?" Rosemary shrieked.

Primrose and Harriet scurried behind a chair and Sable and

Nightshade ran straight up the curtains in fright.

Snowflake spun round and stood on his hind legs in front of Rosemary.

"Missing YOU," he miaowed. "What Wendy means is Coalface is missing YOU."

Snowflake winked slyly at Wendy and secretly blew Sable a kiss as she clung to the curtain pole. There was a scary stillness for a moment.

Rosemary scooped Coalface up and stared into his flashing eyes. He opened his mouth to speak. Snowflake held his breath and wound his tail around Wendy's leg. Then Coalface spat and a shower of saliva hit Snowflake's face.

Rosemary let out an ear-splitting screech.

"He's amazingly angry," she cried. "Marvellously mean. He can come and stay with you again, Wendy."

"Snowflake," Wendy said after Rosemary, Primrose and Harriet had left. "Did Coalface say where he had been?"

"I don't think he'd been far," Snowflake murmured as he washed his face for the umpteenth time.

"He was so cross when Rosemary came to fetch him." Wendy mused. "I almost wondered if he was sad to be leaving us. What do you think Snowflake?"

"You could be right," Snowflake licked his paw. "Coalface is probably going to be feeling a bit blue for quite some time!"